By Anita Nahta Amin, M.S.
Illustrated by Chris Jones

Publishing Credits

Rachelle Cracchiolo, M.S.Ed., *Publisher*
Conni Medina, M.A.Ed., *Editor in Chief*
Nika Fabienke, Ed.D., *Content Director*
Véronique Bos, *Creative Director*
Shaun N. Bernadou, *Art Director*
Susan Daddis, M.A.Ed., *Editor*
John Leach, *Assistant Editor*
Jess Johnson, *Graphic Designer*

Image Credits

Illustrated by Chris Jones

Library of Congress Cataloging-in-Publication Data

Names: Amin, Anita Nahta, author. | Jones, Chris B., illustrator.
Title: The legacy of Rashmi Bazaar / by Anita Nahta Amin ; illustrated by Chris Jones.
Description: Huntington Beach, CA : Teacher Created Materials, [2020] | Includes book club questions.
Identifiers: LCCN 2019024414 (print) | LCCN 2019024415 (ebook) | ISBN 9781644913406 (paperback) | ISBN 9781644914304 (ebook)
Subjects: LCSH: Readers (Elementary) | East Indian Americans--Juvenile fiction.
Classification: LCC PE1119 .A55 2020 (print) | LCC PE1119 (ebook) | DDC 428.6/2--dc23
LC record available at https://lccn.loc.gov/2019024414
LC ebook record available at https://lccn.loc.gov/2019024415

5301 Oceanus Drive
Huntington Beach, CA 92649-1030
www.tcmpub.com

ISBN 978-1-6449-1340-6

Printed in China
Nordica.082019.CA21901366

Table of Contents

DONUTS
RASHMI BAZAAR

CHAPTER ONE

No Time for a Rotten Situation

Rashmi sulked as she followed her parents through the parking lot. It was Saturday morning. Everywhere she looked, children were having fun—except her.

Whiz, ding, ding. Teenage bicyclists stopped to peek into a music store. *Rumble, rumble, bump.* A skateboarder rolled down the sidewalk. On a nearby bench, children munched doughnuts and licked powdered sugar from their fingers.

"It isn't fair. Why do I have to work?" Rashmi complained as she reached her parents' store.

Rashmi Bazaar was the only Indian store in town. Every day after school and on weekends, Rashmi worked there. Her friends got to dribble basketballs, ride horses, and zip-line instead. Rashmi craved adventure too.

But Mom said, "Everyone in our family needs to help, especially today. It's our busiest day of the week."

"One day, you'll inherit this shop. You need experience to manage it," Dad said, fiddling with his keys. *Rattle, rattle, click.* He unlocked the door.

A stench blasted out, forcing them to back away for a moment and cover their noses. Rashmi had forgotten to check the vegetable bins last night.

She sighed and slunk inside, wanting only to escape.

"We'll lose customers!" Mom complained, searching for the smelly culprit.

Rashmi paused, slowly filling with hope. "If we don't have customers, can we leave?"

"No, our customers rely on us," Dad answered. "And we need money to stay in business."

Rashmi frowned. Her parents always worried about money. She had overheard their discussions. Mom and Dad often sent money to relatives in India. The money paid for medical care and schooling. Meanwhile, her parents rarely splurged on themselves.

Rashmi studied her own designer sneakers and swallowed a lump of guilt. "I'm sorry. I promise I'll fix this problem."

She sniffed and followed the odor

past shelves of salty snacks and pickle jars. She and her parents walked past boxes of ripe mangoes, ginger root, and bitter melons.

Trying not to breathe, they stopped and picked through the potatoes, where the smell was strongest. Rashmi wrinkled her nose when she touched something slimy.

Thud, thump, thump. Rotten potatoes tumbled into the trash can.

Rashmi heaved the garbage outside to the dumpster. For a moment, the sunshine kissed her cheeks, just before she shuffled back into her dungeon.

CHAPTER TWO

Chores

It was almost opening time. Rashmi propped the back door open, while Dad started a fan and Mom lit incense sticks. Plumes of perfumed smoke curled up, filling the shop with the scent of sandalwood.

Rashmi reviewed her task list, which Mom had scribbled on a board in the office.

Rashmi still didn't understand why she had the longest list of chores. How could it possibly be an equal split of duties? She debated whether to mention it to her parents. The last time she had complained, Mom had offered to switch jobs—from sweeping to cleaning the bathroom. Rashmi did not enjoy scrubbing toilets.

"Nobody will notice if I only dust once a week instead," Rashmi tried to persuade Mom.

"It only takes one person to spot dust and gossip to friends during teatime." Mom handed Rashmi the duster. "Clean stores attract customers, but dirty stores don't."

Mom grabbed the inventory book off the desk. She bustled around the store, checking which items were low in stock. Dad tallied the money in the cash register.

And Rashmi, groaning with frustration, went to work on her endless list of tasks.

First, Rashmi dusted the stone elephants in the windows.

She swept the linoleum floor.

She organized the spice packets.

She verified that all items were in their proper places.

For the store's background music, she chose bhangra (BAHNG-gruh) songs. Rashmi giggled and bounced to the rapid, rhythmic thumps of the tabla drums. She hopped up and down while flicking her hands like a dancer in an Indian movie.

Just as she started enjoying herself though, Dad switched the music. "We don't want customers dancing down the aisles," Dad said. "They might break something by mistake." So Rashmi endured the slow twangs of a sitar instead.

Rashmi finished cleaning the windows with Dad, with no time to spare. It was ten o'clock: opening time!

As she turned on the electric OPEN sign, she glanced out the glass door.

Across the street, the dry cleaner was fiddling with something in his window. It was a Help Wanted poster.

The poster sparked an idea, which began to mushroom into a plan. If her parents had another helper, they wouldn't need Rashmi's help anymore. If they had another helper, she would be free!

CHAPTER THREE

Help Wanted

Rashmi needed to find someone to take her place! It was the perfect solution to her problem.

She hurried to the office and grabbed a marker. She scribbled "Help Wanted" on a sheet of paper. Now, she was ready to post the sign, but her excitement dwindled.

Her parents probably wouldn't approve of it. They might say they didn't need or couldn't afford another worker. They wouldn't like training someone new, either, not when the store was busy.

She would have to find someone her parents couldn't refuse. Maybe she could find an experienced helper who didn't mind working for free!

First though, she needed to do the impossible. Rashmi had to convince her parents to let her display the sign. She dreaded asking them (more than she dreaded smelling bad potatoes), but she couldn't quit. Breathing deeply, Rashmi marched out of the office, ready to face her parents.

"I have a brilliant idea!" Rashmi said, clutching her sign and following her parents around. "We'll tape this to the window, people will apply, and we'll select the best one!"

"We don't need extra help," Dad said, before a customer pulled him away.

HELP
WANTED

“We don’t have time to train a new worker,” Mom said, stopping to answer the telephone.

Rashmi slumped onto a flour sack, wondering what to do next.

“Pranaam (pruh-NAWM).” A voice greeted everyone from the back door.

It was the samosa chef with a stack of foil-wrapped trays. Samosas were pyramids of fried dough stuffed with spiced mashed potatoes and peas.

"Pranaam, Auntie," Rashmi said. The chef wasn't really Rashmi's aunt. Rashmi called elders "Auntie" or "Uncle" to show respect.

Rashmi set aside the sign to help Auntie unload the trays onto a cart. Auntie nodded at Rashmi's sign and said, "I know the perfect helper."

Flirting with freedom, Rashmi raced to Mom and cried, "Auntie knows someone who needs a job!"

"We don't have any jobs available," Mom said, trampling all hope.

"I understand," Auntie said. "He is new to the country and seems hardworking, so I feel sorry for him. He has a family, too, which reminds me…" Auntie pulled an enameled tin from her bag and gave the gift to Mom. "After my husband lost his job, I tried selling samosas. Initially, no one except you would buy them. Even when your shop was new and struggling, you kept my family afloat. Today marks my tenth year in business!"

Rashmi's mind twisted with surprise. Her parents had boosted Auntie's samosas to fame!

Mom gave a nod of embarrassment. "We like to support hard workers, and your food is delicious." She hesitated with a frown. "Maybe this hardworking newcomer can help here part-time, but we can't pay much."

Rashmi gasped with delight, and Auntie left, smiling.

An hour later though, Auntie telephoned the shop. Her friend had already found another job.

CHAPTER FOUR

Seeking Applicants

"There must be other hard workers needing jobs," Rashmi insisted.

Finally, Mom sighed. "Go ahead. Display your poster. If someone accepts our offer, they really need help."

So Rashmi slapped her sign on the window and stalked the entrance.

Customers streamed through the

shop. She peppered each one with the same question.

"Are you an applicant?" Rashmi eagerly asked a college student. But the student just wanted henna paint for tattoos.

An uncle was interested, until he heard the wages. "My daughter's wedding will be too expensive for that pay!"

One job seeker needed a translator. She didn't speak any of the Indian languages Mom and Dad knew.

Rashmi was losing hope when a gruff man jabbed her sign. He had just finished shoving a tea box into the lentil section of the store. "I'll apply," he said in an impatient voice.

Rashmi blinked, trying to justify freedom at the expense of sloppy help. Ultimately, she couldn't let her parents suffer. She mentioned the salary to drive the man away. He scoffed before leaving. "The dry cleaner pays more."

Finding a helper was becoming

hard work.

Ding, ding. The front door opened, and Mr. Peroni bellowed "Buongiorno!" (bwohn-JOR-noh) as he carried in a pizza box. He owned the pizzeria two doors down and always smelled like tomato sauce.

Rashmi's mouth watered at the thought of his pizzas. "Mr. Peroni, can I switch places with one of your assistants?"

Mr. Peroni chuckled. "I need them, but you can be my volunteer taster if you want."

The invitation brightened Rashmi's day. "I accept!"

Mr. Peroni handed her the box. "Your shop inspired me to make a spicy chicken pizza."

Rashmi savored her treat. "Delicious!"

"I'll name it 'The Rashmi,'" Mr. Peroni said, making Rashmi smile.

He bought his normal lunch: two samosas, a jar of mint chutney, and a

bottle of guava juice. "This is the first place I ever tasted these, and now, they're my favorite meal."

"That is hilarious because pizza is mine!" Rashmi took another bite but stopped chewing when she glimpsed outside.

The dry cleaner was removing his Help Wanted poster. He had already hired a helper, while she was still struggling.

While Rashmi was daydreaming about finding help, someone else quietly sauntered through the door. Magic Uncle was a scientist and mystic. Today, he had brought Rashmi her astrology chart.

"The planets ruined your morning. When Saturn moves here," he explained, tapping the chart, "your day might improve. It depends on a major decision you'll make."

I must find the perfect helper! Rashmi thought. With renewed hope, she continued searching while Uncle and Dad gossiped.

Uncle pointed out an ad for a lawyer in the cultural newsletter. Dad sighed wistfully. "I remember being a barrister."

A barrister was a lawyer in India. Mom had been a barrister too. Her parents rarely mentioned their old careers though.

Surprised, Rashmi asked, "Do you miss it? Can't you do it again?"

Dad shook his head. "The legal system is different here."

Uncle nodded. "Sometimes, one dream ends so another can begin. Leaving family was hard though."

Dad agreed. "Rashmi has only met her grandparents once. Traveling is too expensive."

Uncle and Dad trudged to the office for tea, leaving Rashmi to think. Her parents had sacrificed a lot.

CHAPTER FIVE

Newcomers

When a family came into the store, Rashmi stared. The wife wore a traditional sari dress. The scarlet streak in her hair showed she was married. The husband sported a bushy mustache. They seemed overwhelmed.

But Rashmi could only focus on their son Rohan—he was the new student at school! Busy with her own friends, she had never bothered greeting him.

Rohan's dad greeted Rashmi's parents. "Though I accepted another offer, yours made us feel welcome." He was the worker Auntie had mentioned!

"It can be scary living alone in an unfamiliar country," Dad said. "But now you know us."

Rashmi frowned. Had her parents been afraid while immigrating? She wondered what it was like living so far from family and friends. Her parents had probably felt lonely.

Rashmi wondered if Rohan felt lonely. She made a mental promise to start inviting him to her lunch table.

Dad offered everyone cups of spiced hot milk tea.

"Your shop is like a little India," the wife said, slowly relaxing. "A home away from home."

Silent and with his arms crossed, Rohan appeared nervous. So Rashmi closed the distance and introduced herself. "We go to school together."

"We're schoolmates?" He looked down, scuffing his dusty loafers. "I haven't made any friends yet. The other students think I'm different, but I just want friendship and adventure!"

"That's exactly what I want," Rashmi said excitedly.

Rohan looked up as his face glowed

like a million lanterns lighting up the night.

They wandered around the store, discussing school and hobbies. Rashmi learned that Rohan knew how to play the tabla drum and ride elephants! *How cool!* she thought.

Rashmi and Rohan played games, such as hiding a pickle jar and blind taste-testing, while their parents talked. Along the way, Rohan found and disposed of an empty wrapper and a crumpled receipt. He straightened a shelf sign and held the door open for a customer.

"Have you considered working here?" Rashmi kidded, suddenly stopping as the truth behind her joke sank in. Her choice was obvious! She started to share her decision when the dry cleaner's assistant rushed in, panting with panic.

CHAPTER SIX

A Major Decision

The assistant begged. “My employer hired the rudest helper. I can’t take it anymore! Can I apply for the position?”

“Certainly,” Mom said.

“But I’ve selected Rohan!” Rashmi announced.

“Me?” Rohan squeaked nervously.

“We can’t hire everyone,” said Dad.

Ring, ring! Mom answered the telephone. "You've fired someone, and he's heading over here? We appreciate the warning." After hanging up, she said, "That was the dry cleaner."

The door burst open, and the gruff man from before swaggered inside. "I'll apply for that position. Normally, I choose larger businesses—not unknown holes-in-the-wall, such as your shop. The dry cleaner just fired me for no reason." The assistant quickly slipped out the door and across the street.

Rashmi's heart pounded with resentment. How dare this arrogant man insult Rashmi Bazaar! Her parents had labored endlessly. The shop had helped countless community members.

"This shop is a legacy, not a tiny hole, and the position is filled!" she said.

"Then quit wasting people's time and remove your poster!" he demanded, stomping away.

"I want to help, but I'm not experienced," Rohan said, worrying.

Rashmi reassured him. "I'm not going anywhere. This place is too special. We'll help each other."

So, with all the parents approving, Rohan accepted the offer. His happiness warmed Rashmi's heart.

Mom smiled. "Now that we have two assistants, the vegetable bins should be extra clean," she said.

Rashmi and Rohan looked at each other and giggled. They raced to the vegetable bins. Rashmi smiled as she worked, studying the legacy her parents had built. It had outlasted hardship, sacrifice, and fear.

Would the shop be her legacy too? She wasn't certain, but she would make sure her legacy helped people in need too. It would build bridges between strangers and across communities. It would comfort newcomers who were alone and scared. She hoped one day it would become as important as Rashmi Bazaar.

About Us

The Author

Anita Nahta Amin is an Indian American writer. Her family roots stretch from the peaceful peacock- and camel-filled desert of Rajasthan to the bustling river city of Kolkata. Her fiction has been published in various children's literary magazines. She lives in Florida with her husband and twin children. She enjoys a good cup of masala chai tea and can often be found browsing the aisles of her local Indian shop.

The Illustrator

Chris Jones has been illustrating for children for over 10 years. He has a passion for visual storytelling, and his work can be found in picture books, graphic novels, and magazines. He lives in Toronto, Canada, and reads books with his two children as often as possible.